THE BIG BOOK OF PIRATES

"Where there is a sea, there will be pirates."
—Greek proverb

Adaptation and abridgement by Alissa Heyman
Original Spanish text by Joan and Albert Vinyoli
Illustrated by Xosé Tomás

Library of Congress Cataloging-in-Publication Data

Heyman, Alissa.

The big book of pirates / text abridged and adapted by Alissa Heyman; illustrated by Xosé Tomás; [original Spanish text by Joan and Albert Vinyoli].

p. cm.

"Originally published in Spain under the title El gran libro de relatos de piratas y corsarios."
Summary: A collection of well-known pirate tales, abridged and adapted for younger readers.
ISBN 978-1-4027-8056-1

1. Pirates--Fiction. 2. Adventure stories. 3. Children's stories. [1. Pirates--Fiction. 2. Short stories.] I. Tomás, Xosé, ill.
II. Vinyoli, Joan, 1914-1984. Gran libro de relatos de piratas y corsarios. English. III. Vinyoli, Albert, 1947- Gran libro de relatos de piratas y corsarios. English. IV. Title.
PZ7.H457Bi 2011
[Fic]--dc22

2010015049

Lot #:
10 9 8 7 6 5 4 3 2 1
12/10

Published in 2011 by Sterling Publishing Co., Inc.
387 Park Avenue South, New York, NY 10016
Copyright © 2010 Parramón Ediciones, S.A. - World Rights
Originally published in Spain under the title *El Gran Libro de Relatos de Piratas y Corsarios*
English translation and abridgment copyright © 2011 by Sterling Publishing Co., Inc.

Distributed in Canada by Sterling Publishing
c/o Canadian Manda Group, 165 Dufferin Street
Toronto, Ontario, Canada M6K 3H6
Distributed in the United Kingdom by GMC Distribution Services
Castle Place, 166 High Street, Lewes, East Sussex, England BN7 1XU
Distributed in Australia by Capricorn Link (Australia) Pty. Ltd.
P.O. Box 704, Windsor, NSW 2756, Australia

Printed in China December 2010

Sterling ISBN 978-1-4027-8056-1

For information about custom editions, special sales, premium and corporate purchases,
please contact Sterling Special Sales Department at 800-805-5489 or specialsales@sterlingpublishing.com

THE BIG BOOK OF PIRATES

by JOAN and ALBERT VINYOLI

illustrated by XOSÉ TOMÁS

text abridged and adapted by ALISSA HEYMAN

STERLING

New York / London

www.sterlingpublishing.com/kids

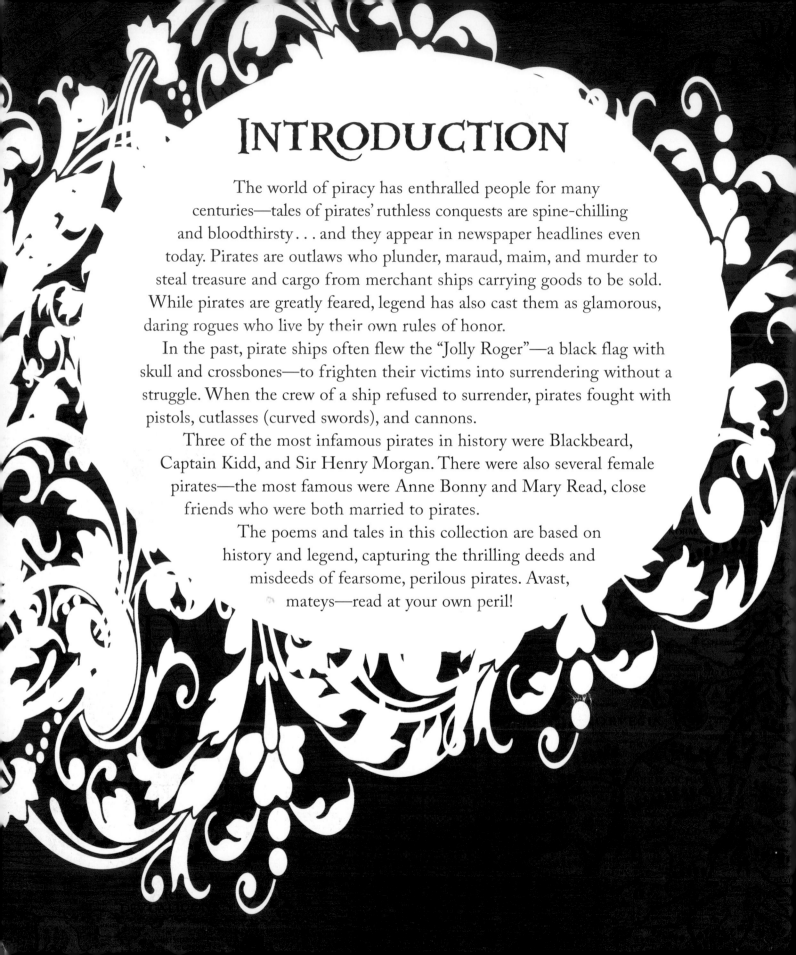

INTRODUCTION

The world of piracy has enthralled people for many centuries—tales of pirates' ruthless conquests are spine-chilling and bloodthirsty . . . and they appear in newspaper headlines even today. Pirates are outlaws who plunder, maraud, maim, and murder to steal treasure and cargo from merchant ships carrying goods to be sold. While pirates are greatly feared, legend has also cast them as glamorous, daring rogues who live by their own rules of honor.

In the past, pirate ships often flew the "Jolly Roger"—a black flag with skull and crossbones—to frighten their victims into surrendering without a struggle. When the crew of a ship refused to surrender, pirates fought with pistols, cutlasses (curved swords), and cannons.

Three of the most infamous pirates in history were Blackbeard, Captain Kidd, and Sir Henry Morgan. There were also several female pirates—the most famous were Anne Bonny and Mary Read, close friends who were both married to pirates.

The poems and tales in this collection are based on history and legend, capturing the thrilling deeds and misdeeds of fearsome, perilous pirates. Avast, mateys—read at your own peril!

from "THE CORSAIR"*
Lord Byron (George Gordon Byron)

O'er the glad waters of the dark blue sea,
Our thoughts as boundless, and our souls as free,
Far as the breeze can bear, the billows foam,
Survey our empire, and behold our home!
These are our realms, no limits to their sway—
Our flag the sceptre all who meet obey.
Ours the wild life in tumult still to range
From toil to rest, and joy in every change.

—◈—

How gloriously her gallant course she goes!
Her white wings flying—never from her foes—
She walks the waters like a thing of Life!
And seems to dare the elements to strife.
Who would not brave the battle-fire, the wreck,
To move the monarch of her peopled deck!

*A corsair is a sailor authorized by an official government to
attack the ships of other nations. Corsair is also used here as
a more romantic way of referring to a pirate.

from "LA CANCION DEL PIRATA"
("THE SONG OF THE PIRATE")

José de Espronceda
Translated by James Kennedy

The breeze fair aft, all sails on high,
Ten guns on each side mounted seen,
She does not cut the sea, but fly,
A swiftly sailing brigantine*;

A pirate bark, the "Dreaded" named,
For her surpassing boldness famed,
On every sea well-known and shore,
From side to side their boundaries o'er.

—◈—

Sail on, my swift one! nothing fear;
Nor calm, nor storm, nor foeman's force,
Shall make thee yield in thy career
Or turn thee from thy course.

*A brigantine is a ship with two masts, and a
favorite vessel of Mediterranean pirates.

THE ROVER

by Joseph Conrad

THE ROVER RETURNS

After roving the seas for most of his fifty-eight years, the old pirate Peyrol returned to his native France carrying a secret. Sewn into Peyrol's vest were the gold and silver coins he had stolen during one of his many voyages.

Wanting rest from his adventures, and not wanting any questions asked, Peyrol left the city of Toulon and traveled into the countryside. He had come home to the same French countryside from which he had run away as a boy after the sudden death of his mother, never returning to France until now.

ARLETTE

Finding an isolated farmhouse on a peninsula overlooking the Mediterranean Sea, Peyrol hid his treasure. The house reminded him of a lighthouse, and he felt that he could stay forever in this sunny, peaceful place.

The daughter of the house, Arlette, was a strange, childlike creature, who flitted about and whose dark eyes never rested, as though she was afraid of what she might see. Peyrol learned that her parents had been murdered during the French Revolution, several years earlier. His solid figure and quiet authority seemed to calm her, and she told him, "I think we shall be friends." Arlette stirred fatherly feelings in him that he had never known before.

From the peninsula, Peyrol could see the English ship *Amelia* patrolling the coast. Napoleon was the ruler of France, and England and France were at war. The English navy had blockaded the French fleet at Toulon.

THE *AMELIA*

The loud blast of a gunshot came from the *Amelia*—some sort of signal. The old pirate Peyrol watched the ship's maneuvers, picturing the captain of the ship as his rival. The English were plotting something, he thought, seeing launches—small boats—being sent from the ship to scout the best locations to attack the French fleet.

THE LIEUTENANT

A young French navy lieutenant named Réal began visiting the farmhouse on his days off. It was not clear why he came, although Peyrol began to notice Arlette staring after Réal. With Peyrol's pirate past, he was unsure what the lieutenant's intentions were toward him, but Réal seemed to like his company. The two men began watching the movements of the *Amelia* together, and the lieutenant muttered strangely, "Papers on a boat. That would be a perfect way."

Meanwhile Peyrol had found a small craft of his own, a weather-beaten two-masted boat on the shore, which nobody wanted because of its bloody history during the French Revolution. Untroubled, Peyrol set to work cleaning and painting it, and then towed the boat into a tiny, hidden cove.

He noticed a change in Arlette. She was no longer a pale, frightened young woman, but seemed full of vitality and life. He realized that she was deeply in love with the lieutenant. He also learned that the lieutenant's purpose in coming to the farm had to do with him.

THE LIEUTENANT'S PLAN

"I have been sent on a mission," Réal told Peyrol. "The object is to trick the enemy and to deceive Admiral Nelson." Admiral Nelson was the famous commander of the English fleet—not an easy man to deceive, thought Peyrol.

"I have papers with false information on the movements of the French fleet. The idea is to send a man out with the papers in a small boat, making sure that he is caught by the *Amelia*. The captain of the *Amelia* will find the false papers and deliver them to Admiral Nelson. This mission must be carried out by an expert sailor." The lieutenant looked at Peyrol. "I told my officers that I have a man for the job."

"A plan to get a person hanged," Peyrol answered. "It will never work."

PEYROL'S PLAN

The lieutenant decided that he himself would be the one to risk his life taking out the boat. Arlette implored Peyrol to save Réal. Peyrol knew that Réal loved Arlette as passionately as she loved him. He sent Réal and Arlette back to the farm while he prepared the boat for sailing, but while they watched from the farm, Peyrol sailed the boat out of the cove himself. Réal realized that Peyrol had taken the false papers and intended to complete the mission alone. The lieutenant was distraught, seeing that he had been tricked. But Peyrol could not let Arlette's happiness be destroyed. He knew what he had to do. He set his boat to meet his rival, the captain of the *Amelia*. Peyrol's heart fluttered in terror at finding himself so close to the enemy.

PEYROL'S TRAP

Peyrol saw that his aim had been achieved. The *Amelia* was giving chase. He led the ship a merry dance, acting in every way like a boat wanting to escape. Ever since he had put his hand on the boat's tiller, all his resourcefulness and seamanship had been bent on deceiving the English captain, the enemy whom he had never seen.

As soon as the ship got close enough, Peyrol knew, the *Amelia* would open fire. The crew would fire the guns because Peyrol knew the captain's mind and knew the captain was a first-rate seaman. *But I*, Peyrol thought, *am just a little bit cleverer than he*. A feeling of peace mixed with pride came over him. Everything he had planned had come to pass. He had meant to play the man a trick, and now the trick was being played.

The captain of the *Amelia* signaled his men to fire. He saw that the white-haired man steering the boat had been hit. "What a seaman that fine old fellow was!" he exclaimed.

The captain delivered the packet of papers found in Peyrol's boat to Admiral Nelson. The English never suspected that the information found on a boat whose sailor was prepared to be shot rather than captured could be false.

A GREAT HEART

Arlette and Lieutenant Réal married and lived together at the farmhouse. One day a vest full of gold and silver coins was found hidden in the well. Nobody but Peyrol could have put it there. They decided to give it up to the government for they realized the coins were ill-gotten goods, but their talk often turned to the man who, coming from the seas, had crossed their lives to disappear at sea again. "He had a great heart," they said, thinking of the old pirate fondly.

END

THE BLACK CORSAIR

Emilio Salgari

NEWS OF THE RED CORSAIR

In the darkness of a Caribbean night, a commanding voice calls out over the sea, "You two men: halt or I'll blow your brains out!"

The men in the wretched wreck of a launch—a small boat from a man-of-war—froze, terrified. They were two middle-aged corsairs, their hats shredded by bullets, wearing rags, and bare-footed, but still armed.

"Who are you? Come on, talk, or I'll smite you both!" the powerful voice continued to shout.

The faces of the shipwrecked sailors in the launch instantly changed from fear to relief. They recognized that disembodied voice.

"Why it's the Black Corsair!" one said to the other.

"Undoubtedly it is he, and we'll have to give him the terrible news of the death of his brother, the Red Corsair, hanged mercilessly on the scaffold in Maracaibo."

"The Black Corsair will take his vengeance. We'll finish off this governor of Maracaibo, the treacherous Duke Van Guld!"

The Black Corsair's big ship, the *Rayo*, which means *lightning bolt*, awaited them.

A man came down from the command bridge. He was dressed all in black. He wore a rich dress coat of black silk, the same color as his pantaloons, tall black boots, and a black felt hat with a large ebony feather.

Though elegant, he was a grim and solemn man, extremely pale. His black eyes smoldered.

"Where have you come from?"

"From Maracaibo, in Venezuela. We sailed with your brother, the Red Corsair."

The Black Corsair took them to his luxurious cabin.

"My brother is dead!" he said sadly. "I can tell from your expressions."

"Yes, Captain, like the Green Corsair, your other brother. The Red Corsair was ambushed. He fought with courage, but they overpowered him and took him to the square to hang him. With the rope around his neck, the Red Corsair spat at the hangman, and then he was hung without mercy. And in a final sign of disrespect, they left him there. He is still hanging in the noose!"

The Black Corsair unleashed a terrifying, heartrending cry that echoed in the darkness. His real name was Emilio Roccanera, Lord of Ventimiglia, and he was known throughout the Spanish Main for his daring attempts to gain vengeance for his family, slain by the deceitful Duke Van Guld, now the governor of Maracaibo.

"Tonight we go to Maracaibo to assault the city and return with my brother's body!"

VENGEANCE IN MARACAIBO

The Black Corsair and his men attacked Maracaibo, and after the fiercest fighting, they rescued the body of the Red Corsair and carried it on a spine-chilling escape through a jungle populated by cannibals, jaguars, quicksand, and strange flora and fauna such as "dynamite trees," which grow fruit that explode when ripe, and "bellbirds," whose calls sound like the bells on sailing ships. At last, assisted by a native who showed them the correct route, they reached the *Rayo*, where they gave the Red Corsair a proper funeral, with the dignity befitting him. They laid him to rest in the sea, as is the custom among sailors.*

"I promise to avenge my brother by finishing off the detestable Van Guld and every member of his cowardly family!" swore the Black Corsair.

THE GREAT SEA BATTLE

From the crow's nest a voice was heard:

"Ship to leeward!"

The infamous Sir Henry Morgan, who was known as the greatest terror of the Spanish Main, was sailing as the Black Corsair's first mate—for the Black Corsair allied himself with the greatest pirates of the era.

The Black Corsair spoke to Morgan. "We will attack and sink the Duke Van Guld's vessel in the same sea where my brother sleeps!"

The *Rayo* turned sharply toward the much larger Spanish sailing ship. On the beams the harquebusiers stared at the enemy ship and the gunners lit their fuses. The Black Corsair and Morgan stayed on the bridge, stalking their prey.

*The tradition of burial at sea has been practiced since ancient times. The body was wrapped in cloth and weighted down so that it would sink, or placed in a casket. The captain of the ship would lead the funeral ceremony.

The two ships were sailing at top speed when a detonation spread out over the waters and an enormous cannonball fell only a few meters off target with a tremendous splash of water. It was a warning from the Spanish ship.

The helmsman of the *Rayo* approached the boarding party with their axes ready and rifles in hand: "Prepare the grappling irons!"

The outline of the Spanish ship could be made out in the darkness: it was a well-armed warship. The Spanish ship sent off another warning shot, which smashed into the end of the spanker gaff, breaking it, and bringing down the Corsair's standard. The third cannonball struck the stern beam, beside the helm. But the *Rayo* drove forward, ignoring the warnings of the other ship, which loomed before them like a monstrous beast.

"Sideways fire!" the Spanish ordered from the big ship and the cannon-balls tore the sails, smashed the beams, but did not hinder the speed of the *Rayo*, which disappeared in the darkness.

At dawn, the Black Corsair decided to aim the *Rayo* straight at the enemy.

The cannon fire began in earnest. The Spanish galleon had three bridges and fourteen cannons. The smaller *Rayo* waited for the right moment to fire its twelve cannons. The pirate ship suddenly veered away with the thrust of a strong blow and then drove its bowsprit in among the ladders and the mizzen rigging of the Spanish ship.

"Board her!" roared the Black Corsair.

There was fierce resistance on the Spanish vessel. The Black Corsair and

his men assaulted the stateroom deck three times, but were forced back. The men fought with cutlasses.

"Surrender!" cried the Black Corsair. "We're not murderers—we guarantee the valiant their lives."

At last the Spanish surrendered, surprised, as they had expected no mercy from the corsairs.

Among the vessel's passengers was an extraordinarily beautiful young aristocratic woman with whom the Black Corsair fell in love, and she with him. After many months of companionship, to his great horror, he found out that the lady was Honorata Willerman, Duchess of Weltrendrem, and the daughter of his sworn enemy, Duke Van Guld. Although torn by his love for her, he had vowed revenge on Van Guld and all of Van Guld's family, so in the end the Black Corsair forced the lady Honorata onto a rowboat and abandoned her to the sea and to fate.

Thus the unhappy Black Corsair gained his vengeance.

END

Bridge

Mainmast crosspiece

Windward sail

Ram

Port

Firearm

Beam

Bonnet

Officers' deck

Bowsprit

Helm

Mizzenmast rigging

Stern roundhouse

Stern beam

Stern

Leeward

Grappling iron

Artillery piece

You can find descriptions of ship terms, types of boats, and crew in the Glossary at the end of this book.

The Queen of the Caribbean

Emilio Salgari

SHIP IN THE STORM

When hurricanes form in the Caribbean, the sea roars in rage, throwing mountains of water against its many beaches. The sun turns blood red. The purple sea threatens with its massive waves.

The few fishermen on the beach of Puerto Limón (a city in what is now the country of Costa Rica) were looking in awe at both the storm and the ship they had spotted on the horizon. "Please protect us!" one fisherman said. "No one would dare to sail on such a dangerous sea except a pirate like the infamous Black Corsair!"

THE BLACK CORSAIR

The fisherman was right. It was indeed the Black Corsair sailing in his ship, the *Rayo*. His friend, the dreaded Henry Morgan, was following in his own ship. The Black Corsair and Morgan were terrifying pirates, although gentlemen of their word. They both lived by the pirate code of honor—sparing the lives of valiant adversaries and always staying true to their promises.

The ship drew nearer despite the hurricane. It looked like a sea bird, clearing the waves gracefully. The fishermen fled to their houses. The ship entered the harbor and dropped anchor. On the forecastle, the roundhouse, and the deck, armed sailors waited while the gunners trained their cannon on the fort in the hills, for Puerto Limón was a garrison town—it had soldiers stationed in its fort at all times.

The great skill of the sailors brought the launches to the beach. A bold man who gave a huge leap to clear the waves was the first of the pirates to gain the shore. He was tall, aristocratic-looking, and dressed all in black. It was the Black Corsair.

One of the pirates said to another, "The Black Corsair is going to look for Don Pablo de Riveira, the attendant of Duke Van Guld. The Duke killed his two brothers—the Red Corsair and the Green Corsair—and the Black Corsair seeks vengeance! Our captain met a beautiful woman, Honorata, with whom he fell madly in love, then abandoned in a rowboat when he found out she was his sworn enemy's daughter. He doesn't know if she is dead or alive, but he claims he sees her on certain tropical nights, rising from the sea in the midst of a strange glow. He cannot forget her!"

TRAPPED IN THE DUKE'S HOUSE

Cautiously, the Black Corsair and his men approached the Duke's house. The house was silent, so they decided to break down the door. A shaky voice shouted, "Enough, gentlemen!"

A tough old man appeared with a sword hanging from his side.

"What do you want of me?" asked Pablo de Riveira, the Duke's attendant.

Instead of answering, the Black Corsair called in his men, who took the house, placing themselves at strategic points.

"Is it true that a Caribbean fisherman told you he saw a rowboat on the waters, sailed by the Duke's daughter, Honorata? Where and when was this?"

At first de Riveira refused to speak, but the Black Corsair threatened the Duke's attendant until he answered. "Yes, a fisherman saw her off the coast of Cuba two days after you abandoned her."

Suddenly a pirate shouted, "Someone's betrayed us. We are besieged! We will have to fight like wild beasts if we don't want to be killed. The Spanish soldiers have taken the street."

"There must be a way out, a secret passage, and you will show it to us, Don Pablo de Riveira," the Black Corsair said, pointing his pistol at him.

"Gentlemen, I am in your hands," the terrified attendant said and led them to a framed painting. De Riveira placed a finger on the picture frame and ran it along the grooves. The picture fell to the floor, revealing a narrow, dark opening.

"Where does the passage lead?"

"It runs around the house and ends in a garden."

At this moment the Spanish soldiers began to surround the house, blocking all exits. But inside the house there was a surprise—the sudden appearance of a young Indian girl, Yara, who declared her hatred for the Spaniards who had invaded her lands and killed its inhabitants. The evil Duke himself had betrayed and killed her family and she, too, longed for vengeance.

Yara told the Black Corsair and his men about a tower where they could find safety. After a tremendous battle with the Spanish soldiers, they managed to escape to the tower. They built a bonfire on the top, a signal that Henry Morgan, waiting in his ship, saw from the bay. Morgan fired a blue rocket, the arranged signal that he would be waiting for them on the beach.

The Black Corsair had been badly wounded in the battle with the soldiers, but he thanked Yara for her great kindness and took her with him in the escape. "For I never forget those who help me," the Black Corsair told her.

THE FIRE SHIP AND
THE QUEEN OF THE CARIBBEAN

There were two Spanish ships closing off the exit from the bay.

"We will prepare a fire ship. We'll fill it with gunpowder, pitch, esparto grass, and fifty grenades," the Black Corsair told Morgan.

The fire ship, loaded like a bomb, was aimed at one of the Spanish frigates and caused such an explosion when it struck the hull that a black cloud filled the bay. Meanwhile, the *Rayo* prepared to sail and veered seawards. The Corsair's strategy had triumphed.

Despite his wounds, the Black Corsair clung to the rail and stared at the sea as if searching for someone. It made Henry Morgan and Yara sad to see him.

"There she is!" he shouted. "Is it her soul wandering still over the sea or is she alive? Oh my Honorata, my beloved Duchess!"

"Sir," shouted Morgan, "are you suffering a hallucination?"

"No, I see her. Look there, her hair is in the wind! She stretches out her arms. She calls to me. Can't you hear her voice? A launch, quick, before she vanishes!" But the Black Corsair then fainted.

The vision of the Queen of the Caribbean had returned to the Black Corsair and would always return. The glistening sea gently rocked the heroic pirates and their tortured captain who was unable to forget the woman he loved—the daughter of his mortal enemy—whom he had let slip away over the shining Caribbean waters.

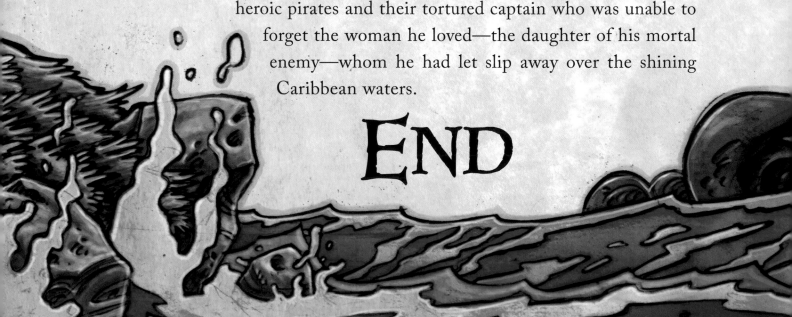

END

THE VENGEANCE OF A HELMSMAN

Soledad Acosta de Samper

THE TWO HUNDRED LASHES

"Two hundred lashes, Lieutenant Bejines?"

"That's what I said."

"Wouldn't it be better to hang the helmsman?"

"I said two hundred lashes!"

"And if he doesn't die?"

"Then send him away on the first boat leaving the city of Cartagena."

"All right, Lieutenant Bejines. I will obey you, but I fear this deed will come back to haunt you."

"Hold your tongue and whip him!"

The helmsman, Iñigo Ormaechea, who was accused of stealing jewels, bore the two hundred lashes. As he was a man of great strength, it seemed that the indignity pained him more than the whipping itself. While he was suffering his punishment, Ormaechea cast a look of such bitter hatred on the lieutenant that Bejines had to leave.

A MASS OF PIRATES

At this time, a mass of pirates crossed the seas to rob and murder anyone they caught unawares. The monarchs of England and France declared they were against piracy, but secretly gave permission for pirates to attack the Spanish ports of South America and the Spanish Caribbean, since Spain was an enemy of England and France.

Robert Baal, a French captain, was in the port of Le Havre, France, preparing an expedition to attack a Spanish colony. His fleet consisted of several well-armed boats, crewed by a large number of criminals who had escaped from European prisons.

THE HELMSMAN

"Captain Baal, I want to enlist on one of your ships," said an unusually strong-looking man, moments before they were about to set sail.

"I don't need you. I already have a lot of strong fellows like you on board," Baal answered.

"But you have no one who knows as well as I do the ports of the Spanish colonies. For many years I was a helmsman and pilot in those places."

"Who are you?"

"My name is Iñigo Ormaechea."

"If you're Spanish, why do you want to attack your own people?"

"That's my business."

"Well I pay no wages and you'll only get a small part of the booty."

"I do not want money."

"You want something else then?"

"Yes. I want you to take me to Cartagena."

"Climb onboard. I am taking a risk in trusting you, but if you are a helmsman as you say, and take us secretly into Cartagena, it will be well worth the gamble."

CARTAGENA

Cartagena, a city in what is now Colombia, was extremely busy with preparations for the year's main festival. Women were putting the final touches on their colorful dresses of velvet, feathers, and gold embroidery. The most renowned cooks were preparing rich, lavish dishes. They cooked all afternoon so as to have less to do the following day. That night, everyone fell into bed exhausted, but very excited for the celebration that awaited them the next day. One by one, the lights went out in every house, until the only light left was one flickering through a window of the cathedral. There was a new moon.

THE WIND GIVES A WARNING

"I hear an odd noise from the sea," one of the residents of Cartagena said, sitting up and calling to his servants.

"Sir," one replied, "it's just the wind rising."

"I thought I heard voices giving orders, and the rattle of weapons."

"It's the wind, sir. It plays tricks on the ear."

"You're right, it's nothing. Let's sleep to be in good shape for the festival tomorrow."

But a little later the city was in grave danger. The French pirates, led by Robert Baal, had slipped inside, taking advantage of the darkness and of the inhabitants' carelessness. Guided by the traitorous helmsman, they had surrounded the city and were preparing to pillage it as they pleased.

THE PRICE OF TWO HUNDRED LASHES

Many were the scenes of horror and terror in the city. Cartagena had never been attacked by pirates before and no one was prepared for such a disaster. The women screamed, the wealthy tried to flee, the bravest searched for their weapons. Priests and friars pled for mercy.

Lieutenant Bejines, who was recently married, was quickly killed by Ormaechea's sword as Ormaechea screamed, "Die, tyrant! This is the price of your insults!"

Iñigo Ormaechea then had to take rapid refuge on Captain Baal's ship, as the people of Cartagena wanted to lynch him in retaliation for his treachery.

ONCE A TRAITOR, ALWAYS A TRAITOR

On boarding Robert Baal's ship, the still enraged helmsman—
unable to get over the past injustice of Bejines despite his recent
revenge—picked up his sword again, went to the captain's cabin,
and took out his anger on Baal.

"Lower a launch, take the men loyal to you, and leave, Captain
Baal. Go to dry land or wherever you want, but clear out before I am
sorry for granting you a few minutes of mercy," the helmsman said,
holding the sword to the captain's neck. "I'm keeping your boat."

"I should never have trusted a traitor," Baal said.

"That's your business. Now your ship is my business."

Two years later, the double-crossing Iñigo Ormaechea was shipwrecked on
the shore of one of the Lesser Antilles—islands in the Caribbean—and was
killed by the natives. Thus the helmsman reaped what he sowed, and in the end
his revenge came to nothing.

END

BLACKBEARD

from *Howard Pyle's Book of Pirates*

THE MOST NOTORIOUS PIRATE OF THE AMERICAN COLONIES

In the eighteenth century, Captain Edward Teach was the scourge of the American colonies. Better known as the fearsome Blackbeard because of the rough, black beard that covered most of his face, in battle he would weave gunpowder into his hair and then set it on fire to make him look even more terrifying. He also added to his menacing appearance by wearing swords and bandoleers—belts with pockets slung around the chest—stuffed with pistols and knives.

At this time, pirates plagued the eastern shore of the American colonies. They attacked merchant ships and stole everything they could. Blackbeard terrorized the coasts of South Carolina, North Carolina, and Virginia, knowing full well that the colonial governments were too weak to protect their inhabitants.

WANTED DEAD OR ALIVE

Nothing was done about Blackbeard until he sailed into Virginia and kidnapped the governor's daughter. Governor Spottiswood offered one hundred pounds for the capture of Blackbeard—dead or alive. The proclamation against the pirates was publicized throughout the colony. Lieutenant Maynard was put in command of the ships that hunted the pirates, and he sailed at once to Ocracoke, North Carolina.

Blackbeard's sloop was lying in Ocracoke Inlet when a captain from another ship told Blackbeard about the price on his head. "Spottiswood is offering one hundred pounds for you, fifty for your officers, and twenty for your men."

Blackbeard scoffed. "You don't think I'm afraid of the governor's bullies, do you? I wish 'em good luck!"

LIEUTENANT MAYNARD

Lieutenant Maynard had already fought Blackbeard near Madagascar, off the east coast of Africa, and won.

"I'll teach that villain Maynard that North Carolina isn't Madagascar. It won't be fit for him to live in these parts if I'm living here, too!" promised Blackbeard.

Lieutenant Maynard's force consisted of thirty-five men in a schooner and twenty-five men in a sloop. He carried neither cannons nor carronades (a short kind of cannon). His schooner's rail was low and offered almost no protection to his men. The rail of the sloop was a little better, but was still not suited for fighting. Maynard was relying on the moral force of official authority to overawe the pirates. He never believed—until the very last moment—that the pirates would show any real fight.

BLACKBEARD'S SHIP

The schooner leading, both of Maynard's ships began to move in the rising breeze. The lieutenant and his sailing master, Brookes, stood on deck. Holding a telescope to his eye, Brookes spotted Blackbeard's sloop three miles away.

"She has a long cannon and four carronades! With our light arms she'll be hard to beat, sir."

Maynard laughed. "I've had many dealings with pirates and though they bluster and make a good deal of noise, when you seize them with a strong hand, there's no fight in them!"

But Maynard was wrong.

Suddenly there was a puff of smoke from the pirate sloop, and then another and another.

"By zounds!" Lieutenant Maynard cried, "They are firing on the boat!"

"It's true, the pirates have fired their muskets!"

"Well, Brookes, you'll have to do the best you can to get closer."

"But, sir," said the sailing master, "we'll be sure to run aground."

THE BATTLE

As Brookes predicted, the keel scraped against the sandy seabed and the schooner soon ran aground. Everything they tried was useless. The ship was stuck.

They were very close now to the pirate sloop. Maynard's schooner was stuck in the mud, and all the efforts of the sailors could only push them close enough to hear a man call out from the rail of the pirate ship. It was Blackbeard himself!

"Who are you?" he called. "What do you seek here?"

The lieutenant kept quiet.

"We're only peaceful merchants," Blackbeard continued. "Come aboard. I'll show you my papers."

"The villains!" Maynard whispered fiercely to Brookes. "Peaceful merchants with a cannon and four carronades, hah!"

When Maynard gave no answer, Blackbeard realized that Maynard was not fooled and stopped pretending to be an innocent merchant.

"If you try to board my ship it will be at your own risk. You have no authority here. If you try to board I'll shoot!" Blackbeard proclaimed.

"Do what you want, but I *will* board your ship," the lieutenant replied.

"If they fired on us now," said the sailing master, "they'd smash us to pieces!"

"They won't fire. They won't dare to."

But Maynard was wrong again.

Almost instantly there came a loud, deafening crash. The air filled with smoke and the sound of wood cracking. There were men down all over the deck.

Maynard heard the pirates cheering from their ship. And he saw that the pirates were preparing to fire the cannon again.

"Everyone below!" the lieutenant shouted. And the deck was quickly cleared of sailors.

BLACKBEARD'S END

With Maynard's schooner trapped, Blackbeard saw his chance to board it, but he didn't notice that Maynard's sloop had been freed and was coming up to protect him. The pirates began to hurl bottles loaded with gunpowder that exploded. Blackbeard and a group of his men boarded Maynard's schooner, leaving only a small party behind to man their getaway.

The sailors and pirates began fighting face to face with guns and swords.

The lieutenant grabbed his pistols and cutlass. He was in the midst of the gunpowder smoke when suddenly Blackbeard was before him, looking like a demon, naked from the waist up and blackened by powder.

Maynard started firing immediately and Blackbeard staggered and fell. Then he was up again, pointing his pistols at the lieutenant's head. Maynard struck blindly with his cutlass. Blackbeard staggered and fell once more, bleeding all over. He got up again and again until he was stabbed twenty more times. At last the swaying figure toppled and fell. Blackbeard lay still, rolled over, then lay still again.

The pirates surrendered quickly when they saw that the mighty Blackbeard, terror of the American colonies, was dead at last.

END

THE BLIGHTING OF SHARKEY

Sir Arthur Conan Doyle

THE ABOMINABLE CAPTAIN SHARKEY

Captain Sharkey in his sinister black ship of death, the *Happy Delivery*, was prowling the Spanish Caribbean again. When other ships spotted the *Delivery* rising over the violet rim of the tropical seas, their sailors changed course. Throughout all the islands, tales were told of burning vessels and dead bodies left strewn upon the sands. All the signs showed that the terrifying Captain Sharkey was back.

It was 1720, and the *Happy Delivery* had lain in wait for three days to attack a ship, but none appeared. Sharkey's violent temper was rising as he sat in his spacious but chaotic cabin, packed with the loot from his raids—valuable pictures, precious objects, furs—everything topsy-turvy. Sharkey was angry at fate itself for not sending a ship his way. Ned Galloway, the quartermaster, a giant bearded man with piercing blue eyes and huge gold earrings, was with him. Captain Sharkey looked like a corpse. He was thin and balding with filmy blue eyes reddened by hate and sea salt. Even brave men would look away from his hunting-dog gaze in fear and loathing.

ON THE EDGE OF MUTINY

Suddenly the cabin door swung open and the boatswain and the gunner of the *Delivery* burst in. In an instant Sharkey was on his feet with a pistol in each hand and murder in his eyes. "How dare you filthy dogs enter my cabin!"

"On a pirate ship we are the officers and we're sick of so much ill treatment at your hands," the pirates answered.

Realizing the situation was serious, Sharkey offered them drinks. They refused.

"Captain, the crew can stand no more and wants to make its own decisions."

Sharkey tried to threaten them, but they convinced him that a mutiny was close at hand and that his life was in danger.

"There are forty men led by Sweetlocks, and on the open deck they would surely cut you to pieces."

SWEETLOCKS

At that very moment a crashing blow fell upon the cabin door and Sweetlocks entered. He was a tall, dark man, with a deep red birthmark upon his cheek.

His outrage was somewhat shaken as he looked into Sharkey's blazing eyes, but then Sweetlocks regained his poise. "The crew believes you are possessed by the devil and that there will be no luck for us while we sail in your company. This horrible calm is caused by your evil deeds. There was a time when we raided several ships a day and had money, women, and drink to our liking. Now, there is only wretchedness and boredom. Also, we know that you killed the carpenter, Jack Bartholomew, and so we go in fear for our lives."

While he talked, Sharkey had stealthily pointed a pistol under the table at Sweetlocks. He was fingering the trigger, when a voice suddenly shouted, "Ship ahoy!"

THE GREAT SHIP

In a flash the quarrel was forgotten, and the pirates rushed to see an enormous ship, with every sail unfurled, passing very close to the *Delivery*. The ship was a merchant vessel, and thus barely armed. Exultation seized the pirates. They fastened the *Delivery* with grappling hooks to the merchant vessel, assaulted it, and eliminated the surprised sailors on watch, while they took control of the sleeping crew. The great ship was the *Portobello*, sailing from London to Jamaica with a cargo of cotton, a thousand guineas in the ship's safe, and rich merchants for passengers. Sharkey's men began searching and throwing overboard most of its occupants with roars of excitement and uncontrollable glee.

DEADLY COURTESY

Sharkey found the captain of the *Portobello*. "One skipper should show courtesy to another," he said, bowing mockingly, "so in good manners I have left you for last!"

The captain replied, "And so I shall go overboard, but before I go I would say a word in your ear. I am not asking for mercy, but telling you what the true treasure of my ship is. It is a young woman of extraordinary beauty, daughter of a count and countess of Spain, Inez Ramirez. For reasons of safety she is locked up near my cabin. I tell you this as a last gift, though why I don't know, as you only deserve the gallows!"

After these words the captain of the *Portobello* threw himself over the rail and disappeared into the sea.

THE BEAUTIFUL PRISONER

The pirate crew, with Sharkey leading them, searched for the prisoner's cabin. They heard shrieks behind a barred door, which they knocked down, and in the light of their lanterns they saw a lovely young woman with unkempt hair and dark, frightened eyes. They dragged her to Sharkey, who touched her with his bony hand, as if marking her as his property.

That night there was a party in the cabin with Sharkey; the quartermaster, Ned Galloway; and Baldy Stable, the pirate ship's doctor. Sharkey ordered the beautiful prisoner be brought before him. Despite the realization of her plight, Inez Ramirez seemed calm and proud, glittering in her elegance. Incredibly, she smiled, a triumphant gleam in her eyes.

SHARKEY'S DELIRIUM

Sharkey sat the woman on his knees. "I will cut the man into pieces who comes between us!" he shouted, looking at the other men with fishlike eyes. Sharkey then asked Inez why she had been locked up on the *Portobello*.

"No Inglese—no Inglese," Inez replied. Then she touched the Captain's face and hair with her hands.

"Sink me if she has not learned to love me at first sight!" exclaimed Sharkey. He pressed her to him and kissed her.

THE POISONED GIFT

Suddenly the doctor, Baldy Stable, cried out, "Captain Sharkey, look at her hand!"

The Captain looked closely at the hand that had touched him. It was strangely pale and covered with white dust. This same dust lay thickly on Sharkey's cheek. With a cry of disgust he flung the beautiful woman from his lap. Her eyes blazed like a maniac's. She sprang at the doctor, who fell under the table. Then she grasped Galloway by the beard, but he tore himself away.

Finally they succeeded in stopping her and returned her to her cabin.

Galloway was the first to speak. "A leper! She has cursed us all!" For the poor Inez had leprosy—an incurable disease that deformed the body and finally caused death.

"She never laid a finger on me," said the doctor.

"She only touched my beard and I will have every hair of it off!" exclaimed Galloway.

Sharkey wiped away the fatal dust that smeared him. "What of me?" he cried.

"The taint is on you," declared the doctor.

THE FINAL MUTINY

The gift of leprosy was the great vengeance of the captain of the *Portobello*. Now Sharkey and his men understood why the most valuable booty had been locked in a cabin. The disease had probably been discovered during the voyage and so Inez had been isolated.

All Sharkey's officers deserted him. None came to his aid. The pirates held a meeting and then Sweetlocks came to talk with Sharkey.

"Captain Sharkey, you have mistreated us for years. You killed the carpenter and you kept the best booty for yourself. Now you are poisoned. We pirates of the *Happy Delivery* have decreed that before the plague spreads, you shall be set adrift in

a dinghy. We grant you the good fortune of being accompanied by your beautiful prisoner."

Sharkey didn't speak, but his baleful eyes cursed them all. Inez looked triumphant and cursed at them in Spanish.

The pirates launched the dinghy into the sea. "Good luck on your honeymoon, Captain Sharkey!" they cried mockingly. A sudden breeze bore the boat quickly away from the *Happy Delivery*, until the sea and horizon swallowed it up.

Some months later, a British warship recorded that a corpse of a woman with the remains of fine clothing had been found near a hut on the island of Hispaniola. There were also signs that a man had lived there for a time, but he was now gone. Whether Sharkey was still alive or not remained a mystery that gave his former crew the shivers whenever they thought of him.

END

THE
GHOST PIRATES

William Hope Hodgson

STRANGE RUMORS

Despite tales that there was something odd about the *Mortzestus*, I signed on to sail with her. People said that she always ran into fierce tempests and had more than once come back with broken masts. Her crossings were curiously long. There were rumors of strange things happening aboard—and that she was haunted. As well, it was curious that the entire crew had cleared out when she came into port, except for one young fellow. "There are too many shadows about this ship. They get on your nerves like nothing I've ever seen before," he told me. But I was eager to get home and willing to take the risk.

A SHIP OF SHADOWS

On a fine night with a bright moon, I was on watch when my gaze fell on the form of a man stepping onboard from the sea. I stood up and stared, but the thing had disappeared into the shadows. I followed, but saw nothing. Then I turned and saw the figure make three quick strides to the rail and step over it into the sea. I rushed to the side and stared over, but nothing met my gaze, except the shadow of the ship sweeping over the moonlit water.

More strange things began to happen. Other mates spotted shadowy figures on board. Sails that had been stowed away broke free in calm weather. A sail thrashed wildly on a windless night, knocking a sailor off the mast. The young fellow who had spoken of shadows gave a frightful scream and fell from the rigging, crashing onto the deck. Sailors struggled with shadowy figures who grabbed them and tried to knock them into the sea. There was more talk of the ship being haunted.

I began to believe that in some way the *Mortzestus* was unprotected, exposed to other elements. Perhaps this ship was naked to the attacks of beings belonging to some other sphere of existence.

THE GHOST SHIP

"See that?" a sailor cried, pointing over the side. "That strange shadow?"

And then I saw what he meant. Something big and shadowy under the water appeared to be rising out of the depths. It was the shadow of a ship, surging out of the unexplored immensity beneath our keel. And then suddenly it was gone. I realized that the ghost ship had been with us all along, and I wondered if the dark shadowy figures that plagued us were the ghost ship's crew. It struck me that whether they were alive or not, they were blood-soaked pirates.

Men began to disappear. There were horrible screams and sounds of ferocious fighting. When I climbed the mast to try to rescue a sailor, something gripped my waist in the darkness with a brutal ferocity. I lashed out with my foot, and it seemed to me I encountered something soft that gave way under the blow. I reached the deck in a blind whirl of fear.

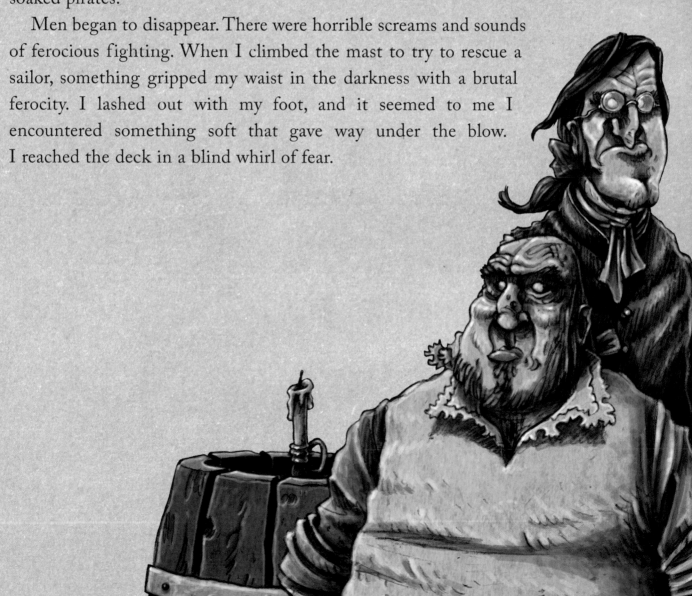

THE GHOST PIRATES

It was dusk, but that did not hide the terrible sight from me. All along the port rail there was an eerie, undulating grayness that spread over the decks. Suddenly, all the moving grayness formed itself into hundreds of strange men. In the half light, they looked unreal, as though creatures from some fantastic dream world had descended upon us. They swarmed over us in a great wave of vicious, living shadows.

Shrieks and cries rose from writhing masses on the decks. With two jumps, I was on top of the deckhouse. I threw myself flat and waited breathlessly. It seemed to me that it was getting darker, and I saw that the ship was enveloped in great billows of mist.

Suddenly, the sails filled out, and the deck of the house upon which I lay tilted forward. The ocean rushed down onto the maindeck. The next instant, the water had leapt to my feet. There was a roar, and I was going swiftly down into the darkness. I struck out madly, trying to hold my breath. There was a loud singing in my ears. It grew louder. I felt certain I was dying. And then, thank God! I was at the surface.

THE DEATH OF THE *MORTZESTUS*

For a moment, I was blinded with the water and the agony of breathlessness. Then, growing easier, I brushed the water from my eyes. I could see the ship's bow plunge right into the water, and I could hear the crying of the lost sailors. The ship slanted more sharply still, and before my eyes, it slid silently into the water, disappearing into the depths of the ocean.

To my amazement, beyond the empty waters where the *Mortzestus* had gone down, not three hundred yards away, I made out a large ship. At first, I could scarcely believe that I was seeing right. Then I started to swim toward it.

A TALE NO ONE WOULD BELIEVE

When I told my tale to the captain of the rescue ship, I said, "There's no one except myself who will ever know what truly happened. People talk about fantastical things happening at sea, but this isn't one of them. This is one of the *real* things. But no one would ever believe it."

And the captain nodded his head in silent agreement.

END

CAPTAIN SINGLETON

Daniel Defoe

KIDNAPPED

I was a little English boy of two, well enough off to have my own nanny. One summer's evening, my nanny took me out and left me alone while she met with her boyfriend. I was snatched away by a woman whose business it was to steal children. For twelve shillings she sold me to a gypsy woman who treated me very well. I called her mother, as she was the only mother I knew. But when I was six, she was arrested and hanged, and I was left with no one to care for me.

THE SEA

A parish minister took me in and told me that, if I studied hard and served God, I might become a good man. It was advice I did not follow. The master of a ship took me under his wing and, when I was only twelve, brought me with him on a voyage to Newfoundland. I went on many voyages with him and grew into a big sturdy boy. But in about the year 1695, our ship was attacked by two Portuguese war ships and taken to Lisbon. My master, my only friend, died of his wounds. I was reduced to starvation, stranded in a foreign land.

EMBARKING WITH THE DEVIL

Fortunately, or so I at first thought, an old ship's pilot took me home with him. After working for him for two years, I embarked with him on a Portuguese galleon bound for Goa in the East Indies.

I learned a little of the Portuguese tongue, a little of navigation, and a lot of how to be a bad sailor and a good thief. As they say, "He that ships with the devil must sail with the devil." Along the coast of Brazil, we exchanged goods for a large amount of gold, and I managed to steal a bit for myself—my first crime. I also discovered that my master had no intention of paying me, only to keep me as his slave. Instead, he began to mistreat and beat me.

My rescue came through no good deed of my own. Indeed, I barely escaped being hanged at my young age. A mutiny broke out on board, and ready to do any mischief, I so openly took part that I was among the men put into irons. But the captain hanged only two mutineers, abandoning the rest of us on the island of Madagascar.

We were at first terrified by the barbarous appearance of the island's inhabitants, but they were a friendly people. We built huts out of tree branches and hunted for food in the woods, often meeting with terrible, wild beasts. But at seventeen my thoughtless, unconcerned temperament made me ready for any daring adventure.

CAPTAIN BOB

We agreed that we would never separate but would live and die together, and that we would be guided by the majority in all things. Our first thought was to escape from the island. Despite being the youngest, I recommended that we build a canoe and search for a larger boat to take over, and then a larger one, until we had one big enough for the crossing. Since we couldn't build a boat safe enough for a long voyage, I thought it better to be a pirate than a castaway. "Young man," the gunner said, looking gravely into my face, "you were born to cause great mischief. Be careful of the gallows."

But the men liked my idea. They began to listen to me. Soon they were teasingly calling me Captain Bob.

And that's how I became Captain Bob Singleton.

THE GREAT OCEAN CROSSING

We built three strong canoes and set out, our odd little fleet carrying more than twenty of the most dangerous men on the seas. A violent storm forced us to land in thick undergrowth, where a sailor had written on a cross, "Point Desperation. Jesus have mercy." When again we set sail, we had the luck to find the wreck of a ship. Working hard, we used parts of the wreck to build our own ship, and then traded the natives little silver and brass figures made by our blacksmith for provisions. As to where we were headed, it mattered little to me; I had no home, and all the world was alike. It was decided to sail toward Africa, and after a long crossing and nearly running out of water, one of our men cried out, "Land!"

THE GREAT LAND CROSSING

Once on shore, we made one of the rashest, wildest, and most desperate decisions a group of men has ever settled upon. This was to travel across the continent on foot from Mozambique on the east coast to Angola on the Atlantic side. I began to take a more active part in our affairs. On being attacked by hundreds of lance-throwing Africans, I took the lead in fighting back, heartening our men. After that, they asked me to be one of their commanders. The gunner taught me all I know of navigation and geography, and filled me with a desire for learning. "Knowledge is the first step to rising in the world," he told me.

We crossed strange, wild country, howling wildernesses, and a vast desert. An African prince taught us how to make houses to carry into the desert for protection from lions and wolves. He put burning mats on poles to chase away wild animals. We encountered ravenous beasts, scorching heat, hunger, and thirst.

GOLD AND IVORY

We also made amazing discoveries: a field of elephant tusks stretching over eighty miles, and a river bank strewn with nuggets of gold. When we had filled our bags with gold, I suggested that to preserve our harmony and friendship, we put everything in a common fund and divide it equally at the end of our journey.

MY PIRATE'S HEART

When we at last reached England, each of us had a small fortune. Having neither friend nor relation in England, I had no one to trust or counsel me, and I fell into bad company. In only two years, I squandered my money on all kinds of folly and wickedness.

For the second time, life made me embark with the devil. I joined with some masters of evil living, with whom I went to sea in an English ship captured by force. My pirate's heart awoke again. Without any pang of conscience, I succeeded in becoming captain of a whole pirate fleet. Flying our Jolly Roger—a black skull and daggers—we captured all kinds of boats and valuables.

One particular capture I considered most valuable was of a Quaker surgeon, a good-humored, brave fellow called William Walters, whose solid good sense I came to rely on. Accounts of our adventures had become so widespread that several English men-of-war had been sent to attack us. William questioned me, "Friend, what does that ship follow us for?"

"Why, to fight us," I said.

"Why then, friend, do you run from her? Will it be better for us to be taken farther off than here?" So we made our stand, surprising and vanquishing them.

We decided to run down the other man-of-war, when William asked me, "Is your business not to get money? So would you rather have money without fighting, or fighting without money? Does not a merchant ship have twice as many riches?" So we left off our pursuit of the war ship. William was right again. He became my trusted advisor and closest friend.

A TROUBLED CONSCIENCE

When we had more than enough money than we needed for the rest of our lives, William talked to me of giving up the pirate's life and repenting. For the first time, my conscience began to trouble me about the criminal ways in which we gained our fortune, and the money ceased to give me any pleasure. We decided to disguise ourselves as Armenian merchants to hide our pirate faces. In Venice, we exchanged all our goods for cash, and William began to speak of going home to England. I told him that the sea was my home, the only one I had ever known. But not wanting to part from him, I finally agreed to accompany him.

A MARRIED MAN

Before journeying to England, we sent a large sum of money to William's sister, his only relative there. She was a poor widow with four children who lived on the proceeds from a small shop. We wrote that she should leave the shop and buy a house near London, telling no one about her new wealth. We reached the Port of London with a cargo of silk, still disguised as Armenians and pretending to know no English. There were many people in England who would have been happy to have our heads.

Hoping to repent for my past life, and knowing I could not return the money to those I had stolen it from, I decided to use my fortune to do acts of charity. A little later, I married William's sister, with whom I am much happier than I deserve. And now, after daring to tell my life's story, I'll say nothing more about the present, so that no one will find out more than I want them to know about your friend, Captain Bob.

END

PIRATES OF THE SPANISH CARIBBEAN

from *Howard Pyle's Book of Pirates*

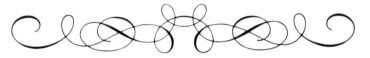

PIERRE LE GRAND

The Frenchman, Pierre le Grand, was the first French pirate of the Spanish Caribbean. Starting in the mid-seventeenth century, French adventurers discovered great numbers of wild cattle, horses, and pigs on the island of Hispaniola (now Haiti and the Dominican Republic), which had been colonized by the Spanish. The French made money selling the meat to ships going to Europe. But Pierre le Grand discovered a quicker, easier way to wealth.

Gathering twenty-eight men and setting out in a small boat, he stormed a Spanish ship containing three times as many men. Bursting in on the captain, who was playing cards, Pierre demanded possession of the ship. The captain had no choice, and Pierre won a great prize. News of his conquest spread, and other brutal men decided that they, too, could seize treasure by becoming pirates.

THE MOST FAMOUS PIRATE OF THE CARIBBEAN

Captain Henry Morgan, a man of great daring, cruelty, and lust for gold, brought pirating to the height of its glory. With a band of ruthless men, he attacked and plundered many cities. After robbing the inhabitants of Gibraltar, Morgan found himself surrounded by three Spanish men-of-war. He offered to relinquish all his plunder if he could go free, but the Spanish admiral refused. The pirates then turned one of their vessels into a fire ship, using logs and leaves soaked in oil. As the pirates fought with the Spaniards, both ships were enveloped in a mass of roaring flames—and the pirates, led by Morgan, escaped!

Now Captain Morgan determined to capture Panama. His men marched through the wilderness, almost dying of starvation, but upon reaching the city, they vanquished the thousands of Spaniards and set fire to the town, destroying one of the greatest cities in the New World. They marched away with horses and cattle loaded with treasures of gold, silver, and jewels, but what became of that fortune only the dishonest Morgan knew—for when it was divided up there was only a small portion of silver coins for each man!

For the amount of damage he brought to the Spanish powers in the Caribbean, Morgan was honored and knighted by King Charles II of England and eventually made governor of Jamaica.

MAROONERS

After Captain Morgan retired, the pirates of the Caribbean declined in wealth and wickedness, swept away by angry governments. But they didn't disappear; they spread out to attack other parts of the world. Among these was the bold Captain Avary, one of the first pirates to be known as a marooner. Deciding to turn pirate, he simply lifted his ship's anchor one night and sailed it out to sea. When the captain awoke, Avary informed him that he was taking the ship to India to make his fortune, and he put the captain on shore. Marooning their enemies on deserted islands and leaving them to perish became a favorite weapon of these pirates.

Avary indeed found his fortune in India, capturing an Indian vessel laden with treasure. Deciding he had enough money to retire on, Avary then cheated his partners out of their share of the fortune. He settled in Ireland, entrusting his jewels to a merchant, who made off with them, being as much of a thief as Captain Avary!

PIRATES COME TO THE AMERICAN COLONIES

Spreading north from the Caribbean, pirate ships began plaguing the American shore. For fifty years in the eighteenth century, marooners cruised up and down the Atlantic seaboard, flying their skull and crossbone flags, and terrorizing people and ships from New England to Charleston, South Carolina. Two of the most infamous pirates of the time were Captain Robert Kidd and Captain Edward Teach, known as Blackbeard.

For many years, Robert Kidd was a pirate hero. There was hardly a stream or sandy beach along the coast where he was not said to have hidden a fabulous treasure. This was all legend, and his great treasure was in fact only one buried chest—if this, too, wasn't a myth.

But Blackbeard was the real thing—a ranting, raging, roaring pirate. He really did bury treasure, make more than one captain walk the plank, and commit many murders.

THE PIRATE BLACKBEARD

Blackbeard got his name because of the large amount of black hair that covered his face. When he fought, he wore a kind of bandoleer from which three pistols hung. He stuck lighted matches under his hat, which lit up his fiery eyes and gave him a fierce, wild look.

Arriving on the South Carolina coast, Blackbeard barricaded the Charleston Harbor, holding all ships and their passengers for ransom. From there, he proceeded to plunder the coast of North Carolina, amassing a huge fortune, which he, like most pirates, was loathe to share.

Blackbeard pretended to accidentally run two of his ships aground, escaping with his riches and forty of his favorite crew on the only remaining boat. Even then, he thought there were too many men, so he marooned twenty more

pirates, thereby doubling his fortune! He then took up the king of England's offer to pardon all pirates who surrendered, and he settled down to a quiet life in North Carolina with his riches. But tiring of this life, he resumed his pirate career, cruising the rivers of North Carolina and terrorizing the inhabitants, until finally they rose up in protest. Two men-of-war confronted Blackbeard, and a fierce fight ensued, with the pirates boarding one ship under cover of smoke. Blackbeard and the ship's captain, Lieutenant Maynard, engaged in hand-to-hand combat. Although shot through, Blackbeard kept fighting until he was stabbed twenty times and took five more bullets.

These fierce pirates are only a few of a long list of wild men whose very names made ship captains tremble and who plagued the shores of the Spanish Caribbean and American colonies in a more lawless time.

END

CAPTAIN SCARFIELD

from *Howard Pyle's Book of Pirates*

CAPTAIN COOPER AND LIEUTENANT MAINWARING

Captain Cooper was a prominent man in Philadelphia, regarded by the townspeople as a model businessman, a peace-loving Quaker, and a responsible family man. His trading schooner, the *Eliza Cooper*, crossed the West Indies. He always succeeded in selling his goods and became one of the wealthiest merchants in Philadelphia.

Lieutenant Mainwaring was a friend of Cooper's. The lieutenant was a frequent visitor to the home of Captain Cooper—he and Cooper's niece were secretly in love—until Mainwaring received orders from the American government to take the *Yankee*, a heavily armed brig, and destroy all the pirates who were sacking the Bahamas.

MAINWARING HUNTS FOR CAPTAIN SCARFIELD

For five months, Mainwaring cruised the waters of the Bahamas. He destroyed many pirate crafts. The name of the *Yankee* struck terror in the heart of every sea wolf. But the pirate whom Mainwaring most sought, Captain Jack Scarfield, remained elusive. Mainwaring always arrived too late, finding only the wreckage and the dead that Scarfield left behind. Lieutenant Mainwaring even found some castaways who had been kept alive solely to give Mainwaring a message—these men were to be served up to the lieutenant "cooked," with Scarfield's compliments. The pirate's taunting of the lieutenant went on until Mainwaring swore, "Either Captain Scarfield or I will soon be dead!"

CAPTAIN COOPER'S SCHOONER

Mainwaring hoped to capture Captain Scarfield on San José, a refuge for pirates. In a bay off of the island, Mainwaring came across a great ship lying at anchor. The lieutenant used a telescope to read the schooner's name.

"*Eliza Cooper*," he whispered. This was the last place in the world he would have expected to find Captain Cooper's ship!

He decided to visit the schooner and found Captain Cooper waiting for him. Cooper's face showed no surprise at this unexpected encounter. Once on board the lieutenant was even more astonished—there were eight twelve-pound cannons!

"I am bewildered, Captain Cooper. Why does your schooner look like a man-of-war?"

"I am a man of peace, Mainwaring, but how do you think I can survive without this appearance of force? The pirates would assault my boat if it just looked like a merchant ship."

Mainwaring was dubious. "Captain Cooper, if it came to blows with such a pirate as Captain Scarfield, would you fight?"

"As I said, I am a peaceful man, but I could not say the same of my crew, if they were harassed by some pirate."

The lieutenant asked another question. "What are you doing in such a dangerous place?"

"I will be honest," answered Cooper. "Pirates are human beings, too, and they

need food as much as any man. I get a higher price selling goods to them. In fact, I was making a deal with my best customer, when the news of your arrival drove him away."

Mainwaring was dismayed. What was his duty? Should he seize the cargo and arrest Cooper for selling to pirates? Before he could decide, Cooper continued. "I know you will ask me about the customer I mentioned. I have no desire to conceal his name—it is the pirate Scarfield."

"What!" cried Mainwaring in disbelief.

"I am no friend of this wicked man. It is only a question of business. I promise to bring you news if I hear anything of Scarfield."

The lieutenant left the *Eliza Cooper* shaken and confused.

THE WOLF IN LAMB'S CLOTHING

Night in the tropics descends with surprising speed. On this night, the darkness fell even more quickly than usual in a velvety, silent blackness. Mainwaring ordered lanterns to be lit and requested a double watch to repel any attack that might be attempted, for he felt uneasy.

Word was brought that Captain Cooper had come to give the lieutenant some private information. Once on board, Mainwaring saw that his visitor was disturbed. "I promised to tell you if I had news of Scarfield." Cooper said. "Are you interested?"

"You know I am! I would rather have news of that scoundrel than anything else in the world!"

"You are in such hurry to meet him as all that!" cried Captain Cooper in mounting agitation. "Very well. Suppose I could bring you face-to-face with him—what then?"

THE GREAT SURPRISE

"I don't understand you, sir," answered Mainwaring. "Do you mean to tell me you know where the villain is?"

"Scarfield sent you something that will surprise you," said Cooper, pulling a gleaming object out of his pocket. It was a pistol, and Cooper pointed it directly at Mainwaring's face.

"I am the man you seek! I am Captain Scarfield!"

Mainwaring would not have been more stunned if a thunderbolt had fallen and burst at his feet. He felt enmeshed in a nightmare. He gazed at Cooper's once well-known, sober face and found it distorted into a diabolical grin, his eyes like a wild animal's.

"You would chase me out of the West Indies, would you? You are caught in your own trap. Speak a word and I'll blow your brains out!"

But Mainwaring reacted with speed and yelled, "Strike him!"

Captain Scarfield—the man Mainwaring had known as Eleazer Cooper—turned around, thinking that another enemy stood behind him. In that instant, Mainwaring attacked. There was a flash of fire as the pistol went off and the pirate emitted a cry. Both men fell together, Mainwaring on top. Quickly Mainwaring got up, roaring to his men, "All hands repel the boarders!" And when the attacking pirates saw Mainwaring, they knew their captain had been overpowered, so they fled.

Scarfield did not die immediately, lingering on a few days more, unconscious. As Mainwaring sat beside the dying man he wondered what it all meant. Could it have been madness that led Captain Cooper to live a double life as a respected businessman and a violent pirate? He would never know.

END

THE FROZEN PIRATE

W. Clark Russell

THE BRUTAL STORM

I have sailed for more than ten years, but I have never seen a storm as brutal as the one that wrecked the *Laughing Mary*. Just before the ship went down, I, Paul Rodney, jumped into a lifeboat—the only member of the crew to survive.

AN ICEBERG

For three days I sailed in my tiny boat through the freezing Antarctic waters, nearly dead with cold. I hardly slept or ate, as it would have been certain death to stop steering the boat for an instant. My heart sank at the thought of the miles of rolling seas between me and land, and the burden of my loneliness nearly crushed me.

On the fourth morning, to my joy, I spotted a line of white coast in the blue distance. I was sure it was land, and that my deliverance was near. But as I approached, I realized that the glassy cliffs formed a mighty iceberg floating upon the dark blue waters, and I was seized with grief at the sight of that great gleaming length of white desolation.

THE FROZEN PIRATE

Finding a cove to land my boat, I climbed onto the iceberg. It is hard to convey a picture of this icy fairyland filled with frozen hollows and peaks, whiteness sparked by the sun into a rainbow of dazzling colors. Walking quickly so as not to freeze, I was stopped by an astounding sight: the figure of a man seated calmly on the ice, like a person lost in thought. His posture was so natural that I was certain he was alive. Approaching him with a mixture of longing and fear, I saw that his eyes were fixed like glass. He looked like a statue—the man was frozen solid!

THE FROZEN SHIP

The man's cloak and boots, combined with his foot-long black hair and beard and his villainous expression, gave him the appearance of a French pirate of the mid-seventeenth century. As gruesome as I found the idea, my instinct for survival was strong, so I decided to take his cloak for warmth, for he certainly did not need it.

Walking eastward, I was again filled with overwhelming loneliness as I looked over those miles of dazzling, unending whiteness. At a hollow, beyond spires of ice reflecting the radiance of the sun, I spotted something even more astounding than the frozen pirate: a ship's masts and sails rising from the ice. In my astonishment, I at first thought it was a mere vision, but on coming closer, I could see that it was a perfectly preserved ship, its entire body encrusted in ice, so that it looked like frosted glass. She was a very old craft, trapped by the ice long ago. Who knows what king ruled England when this vast field of ice broke away from the Antarctic ice cap and floated northward with its captured ship!

THE THAWED PIRATE

The idea of going down into the dark frozen mystery of the ship's interior filled me with dread, but I knew I would die of exposure if I did not. Chopping the ice from the hatch with a knife, I descended into the dark, and, groping with my hands, I touched something which I instantly knew was a human face! Never in all my life had I received such a fright as this. Finding some lights and candles, I saw that seated at a table in the middle of the cabin were two frozen men, facing each other as though they were about to rise from the table.

Shuddering, I quickly left the cabin to explore the ship. I found it stocked with plentiful supplies of frozen meat, potatoes, and cheese. Lighting a fire in the stove with some coal, I made myself the first real meal I had eaten since the wreck of the *Laughing Mary*. As I warmed myself at the fire, I suddenly became aware that the pirate closest to the stove had moved. I watched in fascinated terror as he sighed and opened his eyes, looking directly at me. I realized that he was not dead; his life had simply been suspended at the point when he had become frozen. He had been alive all along! "Where am I?" the man asked, weakly.

THE HUNDRED-YEAR-OLD MAN

I was at first overjoyed to have a companion. He was a French pirate named Jules Tassard. When I explained that he had been frozen for many years and that it was now 1801, he cried out that it couldn't be, for when he had set sail it was only 1753. I realized that he had lain frozen for almost fifty years!

The pirate told me of a treasure hidden in the ship, and showed me ten chests filled with silver and gold coins. We spent hours debating how to free the boat from the ice, for we knew the iceberg was breaking up as it drifted into warmer waters, and we were afraid that the ship would be crushed. But the more I listened to the pirate's stories of plunder and violence, the less I came to trust him, and I became sorry that I had ever brought the vile man back to life.

I realized that the pirate would murder me as soon as we were safely landed so as to keep the treasure for himself, and I worried that I might have to kill him to save myself.

But before that could happen, the pirate suddenly aged overnight. It was as though his true age had suddenly descended upon him. He had gone to bed a man of fifty-six and had woken a man of one hundred and four!

FLOATING FREE

A short time later, the pirate breathed his last, dying of old age, and I felt only relief. Using some explosives I found on the ship, I was able to free her from the iceberg. With the help of the crew of a passing ship, I reached England, where I now live comfortably with my wife and children on the treasure from that horrible land of endless ice and frozen pirates—a place I will never forget!

END

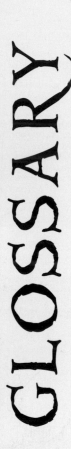

GLOSSARY

SHIP TERMS

- **Artillery pieces**: Firearms or cannons.
- **Beam**: The width of a ship at its widest point.
- **Bonnets**: Canvas sometimes added to a ship's sails to make them bigger.
- **Bow**: The front of a ship.
- **Bowsprit**: A spar projecting from the bow used to anchor sails and other rigging.
- **Bridge**: An elevated platform that houses a ship's command center.
- **Forecastle**: The forward part of a ship, often containing the sailors' living quarters.
- **Grappling irons**: Sticks with a metal tip and hook used for approaching or pushing off another ship.
- **Hatch**: The cover of an opening in the ship's deck leading to a lower deck.
- **Helm**: The wheel or tiller controlling a ship's rudder.
- **Hull**: The frame or body of a ship.
- **Keel**: A large beam around which the hull of a ship is built, running in the middle of the ship, from the bow to the stern.
- **Leeward**: The direction that the wind is blowing toward.
- **Mainmast**: The tallest mast on a ship.
- **Mizzenmast**: The third mast from the bow.
- **Port**: The side of the ship on the left when facing forward.
- **Ram**: An iron tip put on the bow of a boat and used for ramming.
- **Rigging**: The system of ropes and chains used to work the masts and sails.
- **Rudder**: A vertical plate or board for steering a boat.
- **Spanker gaff**: A fore-and-aft sail attached to a spar.
- **Spar**: A pole used to support various pieces of rigging and sails.
- **Standard**: A flag or banner.
- **Starboard**: The side of the ship on the right when facing forward.
- **Stern**: The rear part of a ship.
- **Tiller**: A bar or handle for turning a boat's rudder.
- **Topsail**: The second sail on the main mast.
- **Windward**: The direction that the wind is blowing from.

TYPES OF BOATS

- **Brig**: A two-masted sailing boat.
- **Dinghy**: A small open boat (now usually made of rubber and inflatable) carried on a larger ship to use as a lifeboat.
- **Fire ship**: A ship loaded with flammable materials and explosives, aimed at enemy ships to set them on fire.
- **Frigate**: A fast-sailing warship built between the seventeenth and mid-nineteenth century.
- **Launch**: A small boat, usually with a deck and two masts.
- **Man-of-War**: The most powerful type of armed ship from the sixteenth to the nineteenth century.
- **Schooner**: A slender boat with two or more masts.
- **Sloop**: A single-masted sailing boat.

CREW

- **Boatswain**: The officer in charge of the sails, riggings, anchors, and cables on a ship.
- **Bosun**: Another name for a boatswain.
- **Buccaneer**: A seventeenth century pirate who preyed on Spanish shipping in the West Indies. The name comes from "buccanning" or curing meat.
- **Captain**: The officer in command of a ship.
- **Corsair**: A sailor authorized by an official government to attack the ships of other nations.
- **Gunner**: A sailor working with the ship's cannon.
- **Harqubusier**: A crew member armed with an arquebus (an old kind of rifle).
- **Helmsman**: A person who steers a ship.
- **Lieutenant**: A naval officer ranking next below a lieutenant commander.
- **Lookout**: A sailor watching from the top of the topsail (the second sail on a mast).
- **Pilot**: A person qualified to navigate a ship through dangerous waters.
- **Privateer**: The commander of a privately owned ship authorized by an official government to attack and capture enemy vessels.
- **Sailor**: A person who works on a ship as a crew member.
- **Sea wolf**: A mariner or seafarer, old and experienced in his trade.

GALLERY

Peyrol
The Rover
Joseph Conrad

**The Black Corsair
(Emilio Roccanera)**
The Black Corsair
Emilio Salgari

Honorata Willerman
The Queen of the Caribbean
Emilio Salgari

Iñigo Ormaechea
The Vengeance of a Helmsman
Soledad Acosta de Samper

Blackbeard (Captain Teach) / Lieutenant Maynard
Blackbeard   Howard Pyle

Captain Sharkey
The Blighting of Sharkey
Sir Arthur Conan Doyle

Sailors on the *Mortzestus*
The Ghost Pirates
William Hope Hodgson

Bob Singleton
Captain Singleton
Daniel Defoe

Pierre le Grand / Captain Kidd
Pirates of the Spanish Caribbean   Howard Pyle

Captain Cooper
(aka Captain Scarfield)
Captain Scarfield
Howard Pyle

Lieutenant Mainwaring
Captain Scarfield
Howard Pyle

Jules Tassard / Paul Rodney
The Frozen Pirate   W. Clark Russell

BIOGRAPHIES

Soledad Acosta de Samper (1833–1913) lived in Colombia and overcame many obstacles to become one of the most beloved writers of her day. She began working as a journalist and later went on to run her own magazines, in addition to writing novels and histories.

Joseph Conrad (1857–1924) was born in Poland, but later moved to Great Britain. He wrote in English and is known as one of the best writers of modern literature. He was a sailor for many years, working for European merchants. The places he went and the people he met on his voyages would often turn up in his writing. Among Conrad's most famous works are *Heart of Darkness*, *Lord Jim*, and *The Secret Agent*. *The Rover* was Conrad's last novel, published in 1923.

Daniel Defoe (1659–1731) is best-known today for his 1719 novel *Robinson Crusoe*. It was so popular in its time that some even consider Defoe, born Daniel Foe, one of the first great English novelists. Other beloved works of his include *Moll Flanders* and *Journal of the Plague Years*.

Sir Arthur Conan Doyle (1859–1930), born in Scotland, is best known today as the creator of the character Sherlock Holmes, the most famous detective in English literature. He also wrote many historical novels, plays, nonfiction, poetry, and even science fiction stories. Like Holmes's best friend, John Watson, Doyle was a doctor.

William Hope Hodgson (1877–1918) grew up in poverty and spent his teenage years as a sailor. He was inspired to become a writer by famous adventure authors Edgar Allan Poe, Jules Verne, and Sir Arthur Conan Doyle, and his own writing became highly praised as well, especially the novels *The House on the Borderland* and *The Night Land*. He is considered one of the founding writers of the modern horror and science fiction genres.

Howard Pyle (1853–1911) was a well-regarded illustrator, as well as a writer for children. He famously adapted *The Merry Adventures of Robin Hood* for young readers. *Howard Pyle's Book of Pirates* was a collection of pirate legends and drawings, published after his death.

W. Clark Russell (1844–1911) was born in New York City and became a journalist after eight years as a sailor. His many seafaring adventure stories include *Captain Fanny*, *The Sea Queen*, *The Frozen Pirate*, and *The Convict Ship*. Among his fans was Sir Arthur Conan Doyle, who mentioned him in a Sherlock Holmes story.

Emilio Salgari (1862–1911) wrote many swashbuckling tales of adventure, including his popular series about Sandokan, the Tiger of Malaysia, and his series about the Black Corsair and Captain Henry Morgan. Only a few of Salgari's books have been translated into English from his native Italian, although they have been made into movies, television cartoons, and comic books.